W9-AGD-283

13th STREET

Clash of the Cackling Cougars

Read more 13th Street books!

HARPER **Chapters**

13th STREET

Clash of the Cackling Cougars

by **DAVID BOWLES**

illustrated by **SHANE CLESTER**

HARPER
An Imprint of HarperCollinsPublishers

To Salt, Kimi, and all the other cackling cats who've hypnotized me into feeding and petting them down the years.

13th Street #3: Clash of the Cackling Cougars
Copyright © 2020 by HarperCollins Publishers
All rights reserved. Printed in the United States of America.
No part of this book may be used or reproduced in any manner whatsoever
without written permission except in the case of brief quotations embodied
in critical articles and reviews. For information address HarperCollins
Children's Books, a division of HarperCollins Publishers, 195 Broadway,
New York, NY 10007.
www.harperchapters.com
Library of Congress Control Number: 2020934032
ISBN 978-0-06-294786-4 — ISBN 978-0-06-294785-7 (pbk.)
Typography by Torberg Davern and Catherine Lee
20 21 22 23 24   PC/LSCC   10 9 8 7 6 5 4 3 2

First Edition

CONTENTS

CHAPTER

1

SKI LIFT SCARE!

Ivan watched the light snow falling on the mountain. The only thing he enjoyed more than reading was skiing. His long arms and legs were always graceful going down the slopes. Every Thanksgiving, his mom and dad brought him to a resort. A wonderful family tradition.

This year, his cousins had tagged along.

It had been three months since they'd escaped 13th Street. Malia and Dante thought they were safe now, but Ivan wasn't so sure. He had been doing lots of research, trying to figure out what had happened and why.

But nothing made sense just yet.

"I kind of wish we were back at the lodge with our *tíos*, sitting by that fireplace," Dante groaned as the ski lift wobbled a bit.

"But the view is amazing," Ivan said,

pointing at the landscape.

Malia rolled her eyes at Dante, who was shivering. "If you would just pull up the hood of your parka . . ."

"And mess up this gorgeous hair?" Dante gave her a shocked look. "It took me thirty minutes to get it perfect."

"I don't know how you plan to snowboard down the mountain like that," Malia said.

"Slowly," Dante replied. "Really slowly."

Just then, a humming and creaking sound echoed above the soft whistle of the wind. The ski lift shuddered. Ivan's heart skipped  a beat in fear. What if, somehow, they got trapped on 13th Street again and had to fight more monsters?

Ivan looked up the slope. Coming down toward them was another lift, full of people returning to the lodge. For a moment, he breathed a sigh of relief. Then the other group passed them, and Ivan gasped in surprise!

Sitting in between two kids was . . . Doña Chabela!

She smiled and winked at him.

"Guys," Ivan said. "It's *her*!"

CHAPTER

2

SLIPPERY SLOPE!

Malia and Dante stared at Ivan in disbelief.

"You're imagining stuff," Malia said. "That was just a bunch of tourists."

"It was Chabela Aguilar." Ivan's voice was more serious than usual.

Dante shrugged. "Maybe the cold and snow are messing with your eyes, dude. Three months have passed. Thirteenth Street is over."

"Yeah," Malia agreed. "Let it go."

The lift groaned to a stop. The cousins hopped out.

Ivan gestured toward the ski lift. "Seriously, I saw her."

Dante sighed. "Why would she be in Utah, dude?"

"To make us go back!" Ivan said. At moments like this, he felt like his cousins didn't listen to him.

Malia smirked. "There's no way a portal to 13th Street is waiting for us in the mountains of Utah!"

Maybe I can show them what I mean, Ivan thought. He took his backpack off and pulled out a notebook. "What if Chabela *made one?* I've been doing some research."

"And here we go," muttered Dante, rubbing his face. "Nerd stuff from the Brain."

Ivan's cheeks turned red with embarrassment. He knew Dante was only joking, but it hurt his feelings. Didn't Dante and Malia understand him at all?

Ivan pressed on anyway. He pointed at

pages where he had made drawings and jotted down information. "Look. The symbol we found on open doors? It's the number thirteen, written in ancient Mayan. The two spells we learned from Yoliya, the ghost girl who helped us battle the bats? Also Mayan!"

"So what, you think Chabela is a Mayan witch or something?" asked Dante.

"No way that street's Mayan," Malia muttered.

Ivan shoved his notebook back into his bag. "Fine. Whatever."

I kind of wish I were alone on this mountain, he thought.

Malia frowned. "What's the matter with you?"

"Yeah, you're being weird, Ivan," Dante said.

"I am **NOT** weird," Ivan said sharply.

"You're right. You're actually lucky," Dante said. "Your parents are so cool. My  mom would never let us go snowboarding by ourselves."

Malia chuckled. "Yeah, she'd hold your hand all the way down the mountain."

Ivan sighed. "Can we just go already?"

"Cheer up, dude!" Dante said. "There's hot chocolate at the end of this slope!"

The cousins strapped on their boards and skis, and off they went.

As the cold air whipped his face, Ivan tried to do what Dante had asked and forced a smile. It was almost hypnotic, all the white snow, the gentle slope. He glanced down at his skis, flexing his knees a little, and he felt better.

But then his cousins started to scream!

Ivan looked up just in time to see a portal looming in front of him, swallowing Dante and Malia.

CHAPTER

3

CACKLING COUGARS!

SCRAAAAAAPE!

Ivan's skis grated against the pavement as he passed through the portal into the gloomy world of 13th Street. He slowed to a stop and looked at his cousins.

Dante had fallen flat on his back. Malia was unstrapping her board from her boots.

Behind Ivan, the portal disappeared.

WHOOSH!

"Um, y'all were saying?" snapped Ivan.

"Yikes, sorry, dude. Now we're back at our last checkpoint," Dante said.

"Excuse me?" Malia asked.

"Like a video game," Dante said. "It's the last place we 'played,' remember?"

Malia pointed at the crooked and spooky warehouses that loomed all around. "This is no game, pretty boy."

Ivan pushed down on his right heel lever with a ski pole. "Wonder what creatures we'll face this time."

Malia's eyes suddenly went wide.

"Um, cougars," she said.

"Where?" Dante didn't even try to hide the panic in his voice.

Ivan pulled his boots from his skis and turned around. Slinking up the street were a dozen big, tawny cats. Some of them stood on their hind legs, gripping spears in their front paws!

"Hey, troop!" the lead cougar called. "Knock, knock!"

"Who's there?" the rest shouted in unison.

The cousins stared at one another, mouths open.

"Talking cougars," Ivan muttered. "*That's new.*"

"Kids," the cougars' leader replied.

"Kids who?"

"Kids who're not supposed to be here!" the cougar shouted.

The entire troop erupted into cackling laughter.

Dante stood up and grabbed his board. "That was a terrible joke."

"Funky breath. Ferret fire. Now . . . dad jokes? Seems like a step down," Malia said.

One of the big cats stood. "Ooh, I've got one, pals. Why did the human throw a clock out the window? Because it wanted to see time fly!"

The cougars grabbed their bellies and guffawed. Some even rolled around in the street, howling with laughter.

Suddenly, Ivan felt sick to his stomach. Dante held his hand to his mouth for a second, then rushed off to puke.

The cougars kept laughing, but now their chuckles sounded kind of mean. And they were trotting faster, closing in.

Malia dropped to her knees. "Their laughter . . . it's making us . . . sick. We need . . . to run . . . but I'm so dizzy."

Another cougar shouted, "Why did the human put its money in the freezer? It wanted cold hard cash!"

The cackling of the cougars was impossibly loud! Ivan could hardly think.

Dante grabbed Malia's arm and pulled her to her feet.

"Come on, Ivan!" he screamed. "We have to get away!"

Ivan's cousins began to hurry up the street. Their bulky snowsuits and boots made it hard to run. Ivan tried to follow. But the cougars' laughter began to fill up his head. The tall, slanted buildings seemed to swirl all around him. His long legs got tangled up, and he tripped.

In seconds, he was surrounded by snarling cougars. He couldn't lift his head to look at their faces. But closeup, he made out two strange symbols on metal bands around their ankles.

The lead cougar leaned close to Ivan, its breath hot on his ear. "Go catch your friends," it whispered.

Ivan felt himself standing. He couldn't stop himself. His long arms stretched out, fingers hooked like claws.

The cougars' laughter had hypnotized him!

Then he started running after his cousins, ready to grab them!

¡Muy bien! You've read three chapters. Nothing funny about that!

CHAPTER

4

SWALLOWED BY A CYPRESS!

The cougars' laughter echoed in Ivan's head, making him run faster. The street became an avenue with thick, leafless trees on either side. A part of Ivan's mind recognized them as Montezuma cypresses.

Within seconds, he was almost on top of his cousins.

"Ivan!" Dante shouted. "What are you doing?"

Ivan tried to answer, but his lips wouldn't move. His fingers had nearly snagged the hoods of their parkas when something yanked him back.

Vines had wrapped around him! They were pulling him straight toward a thick trunk!

Just as Ivan was about to smash into the cypress, it **OPENED UP**!

THWACK!

He was trapped. The inside of the tree was dark. From outside came the muffled voices of cougars.

"Where'd they go?"

"No clue! It's like they vanished, Captain."

Suddenly, a light seemed to switch on. Just inches away from Ivan stood a strange being. It had green skin and mossy hair. In its hands was a green stone.

Jade, Ivan thought. *But glowing and held by a . . . tree elf?*

The tree elf pressed the stone to Ivan's heart. "Heal up, Shi-PAH-ti!" it whispered.

Warmth spread through Ivan's chest. The laughing echoes in his brain stopped. He found he could control his movements again.

The elf pulled its hands away. They were empty.

"Where did it go?" Ivan asked, glad to hear his own voice at last.

"Broke spell. Then vanished. So healing stones work," the elf replied. "Find the park. Should be safe."

The tree opened up. Ivan stumbled out into the gloom of 13th Street.

"Wait!" said Ivan, turning back. "How do I stop the cougars from hypnotizing—"

But the tree had closed up.

Suddenly, Ivan remembered the earmuffs

hanging around his neck. He pulled them up over his ears.

That was why he didn't hear his cousins shouting his name.

CHAPTER

5

PAUSING IN THE PARK

Somebody slapped him on the shoulder. Startled, Ivan let out a yelp and spun around.

It was Dante and Malia. Ivan pulled down his earmuffs.

Malia pointed at the trees. "What was that, Ivan?"

"The cougars," he explained. "Their laughter doesn't just make you sick. It controls your mind!"

Dante shook his head. "Not the hypnotism, dude. **THE BIG TREES THAT JUST SWALLOWED BOTH OF US WHOLE!**"

"You didn't see the elf?" Ivan asked. They looked at him blankly. "I'll explain later. There's supposedly a park up ahead. Earmuffs up, just in case."

The cousins set off at a run. A few yards ahead, the warehouses disappeared, replaced by sheer rock and trees, and a path that wound through muddy, dead grass.

Only on 13th Street could a park look this horrible,
Ivan thought.

The three kids stopped and looked back.
No cougars.

Dante's lips were moving. Ivan pulled his
earmuffs away from one ear.

"Excuse me?" he said.

"How'd you snap out of it?" Dante asked.

"Inside my tree was a little green creature, like an elf. It used a glowing stone to break the spell."

"I knew it!" Dante shouted. "Just like powering up in video games. We need to keep an eye out for more."

"Jades or elves?" Ivan asked.

"Both, duh!" Malia replied. "The elves hid us till the cougars went away. They might help us again."

The cousins started walking toward some woods that spread before them on the far side of the park. They tried thinking of options for defeating the cougars.

"Maybe taping their mouths shut?" Dante wondered.

"Good luck getting close to their mouths," Malia responded. "Even with earmuffs on to keep their cackling out of your head, those were some big teeth."

"And spears," Dante added. "They looked like warriors or something."

Ivan snapped his fingers and pulled his journal out again. "Those symbols on the cougars' leg bands. I've seen them before." He flipped through the pages and then pointed.

"The Maya used to name their days with a number and a glyph, a special symbol that stood for a word. I copied them down. Those two mean . . . Yikes."

"What?" Malia demanded.

"One is *ruler* or *lord*. The other is . . . *death*."

Dante bit his lip. "This is the Underworld, isn't it?"

Ivan swallowed hard. "Sure would explain all the zombies and ghosts and skeletons."

Malia took a deep breath. "If we're in the land of the dead, why are there cars and buildings?"

"Because I made them," an unfamiliar voice said.

The cousins spun around to see a figure on the path behind them.

CHAPTER

6

THE QUIET PRINCE

Malia lifted her snowboard like a weapon. "Who are you?"

A young man stepped closer. He looked about thirteen years old. He was wearing a cape of black feathers that made a whispery sound as he moved.

"I'm Mickey Aguilar," he said.

Dante snapped his fingers. "The message I saw on the zombies' warehouse! 'Protected

by Lord Micqui, the Quiet Prince.' That's you, huh?"

"Guilty as charged. And I *do* try to protect people," Mickey said. "Like you kids. Let me guess. The cougars found you."

"Yes," Ivan replied. "They hypnotized me."

The Quiet Prince cocked his head. "Did Shopal save you? Little green guy, likes trees?"

Ivan nodded. "Did you send him?"

"*Más o menos*," Mickey said. "More or less.

I sensed a portal opening near the park. Shopal decided to scout ahead in case the cougars tried to obey."

"Obey what?" Malia asked.

"It's a little embarrassing. They're, uh, following orders," Mickey explained, looking sad. "You see, they're my knights."

He lifted his left hand. Ivan had a sinking feeling in his chest.

The Quiet Prince had a metal band around his arm. It was inscribed with the same scary symbols as the cougars'.

¡Eso! Three more chapters down! You're really moving now!

CHAPTER

7

YOUR BASIC BACKSTORY

Dante lifted his snowboard. "You jerk! You ordered them to catch us!"

Mickey sighed. "Not quite, but they didn't understand me."

Ivan could relate to that!

Malia jabbed her snowboard at Mickey's stomach. "Then why don't you, I don't know, **GIVE THEM NEW ORDERS**?"

The Quiet Prince shook his head. "They're a little dense and pretty literal. They won't accept new orders until they complete the first ones."

Ivan narrowed his eyes at Mickey. "We need answers. Where are we? Why are we here?"

With a moan, Mickey dropped onto a nearby park bench. "It's a long story."

"You better sum it up fast." Malia crossed her arms.

"Okay. Five years ago, my parents went to buy a house closer to my dad's new job.

I didn't want to go, so I stayed behind with my dog, Bruno, at my grandma's house in Gulf City."

Suddenly, things lined up in Ivan's brain. "Wait. Your last name is Aguilar. Is your grandmother Doña Chabela?"

Mickey's eyes went wide. "How do you know that?"

Malia slammed her snowboard down. "Because she's tricked us into coming here *three times*!"

The Quiet Prince pressed his fingers to his temples. "I'm so sorry. I never meant for this to happen."

Ivan sat down beside him. "What happened exactly?"

Mickey's eyes were red. "Bruno ran out of our house one day. A car hit him. I was so sad. And Grandma . . . she has all these books on magic and the Underworld. I started reading."

Ivan nodded. Reading also helped him make sense of confusing things.

"An idea came to me," Mickey continued. "My dad trained me to code on computers. Maybe I could combine technology and magic, make a doorway into the land of the dead, and find Bruno."

Dante's voice trembled. "And it worked."

The Quiet Prince nodded. "Kind of. I peeled off a piece of the Underworld, trapping Bruno inside. I tried to program the place to look like the city streets he knew, so he wouldn't be scared. Then . . . something went terribly wrong."

"You can say that again," muttered Malia.

"We have more questions, dude," Dante said.

"Like why your knights are after us!" Ivan exclaimed.

The cousins were so distracted by the guilty look on Mickey's face that they didn't notice the dozen cougars that had just surrounded them.

CHAPTER

8

NICKED BY THE KNIGHTS!

"Boo!"

Ivan jumped up at the sound. Cackling cougars had made a circle all around them— they were trapped!

Malia reached for her snowboard. "Call them off, Prince!"

Mickey leaped to his feet. "Already told you: I can't! But trust me. I'll get you free."

Then he wrapped his cape of black feathers around himself and disappeared!

"I didn't see that coming," Dante said.

Once the cougars began laughing, the cousins dropped to their knees, they were so dizzy.

Ivan shook his head and pulled up his earmuffs. He helped Malia do the same.

A small but quick cougar pounced at them, snatching Dante's earmuffs with its claws and rushing away.

"Dante, quick! Pull up your hood!" Malia shouted.

But Dante moved too slowly.

"My hair!" he complained. "It took me forever to get it perfect!"

Dante's delay cost him. Ivan could see his cousin's eyes glaze over as the cackling got louder. The lead cougar pointed at Dante and said something Ivan couldn't hear. Then Dante reached out and yanked his cousins' earmuffs down!

As the Knights of the Quiet Prince laughed, their leader smiled, showing its fangs.

"I am Captain Kamak," the cougar declared. "And you are my captives."

CHAPTER

9

THE WEIRD WOOD

Hypnotized, the kids were forced to march. The park path led into the spookiest woods Ivan had ever seen. Strange glowing eyes stared at them from the dark. A few healing stones twinkled among the dead leaves.

A moth the size of Ivan's hand landed on his face. He wanted to scream, but couldn't. He marched on silently, just like his cousins.

Bad jokes kept coming, making things creepier. Strange grunts answered the cougars' cackling. The knights laughed even harder.

There was a rustling sound in the trees to Ivan's left. He couldn't turn to look. All he saw was a strange blur and then a smoky mist that wrapped all around him and his guards.

It smelled like catnip.

Ivan's two cougar guards dropped to the ground, snoring. Then a pair of arms grabbed him off the path.

Something pressed against his chest. "Heal up, Shi-PAH-ti!"

Mickey was using a healing stone on him. Ivan's mind cleared fast. The Quiet Prince pulled him behind a tree.

"Not a word," Mickey ordered.

The Knights were shouting and growling. Captain Kamak started snarling orders.

"It's His Bratty Majesty! You four, with
me! We'll take the prisoners to the camp.
The rest of you, capture the boy cub!"

Mickey yanked on Ivan's parka. "*Vamos.*
Time to move, little bro."

Ivan pushed him away. "They have my
cousins!"

"I'm sorry." Mickey rubbed his eyes. "I'm a
prince with a useless, single-minded army."

Ivan pointed back toward the path. "What command could take *five years* to obey?"

"'Find Bruno,'" Mickey said, "'no matter what. Use everything and everyone you can.'"

¡Excelente! You're about to hit double digits—nice!

①②③④⑤⑥⑦⑧⑨○○○○○○

CHAPTER
10

FURIOUS FOREST

The knights came crashing through the undergrowth. Mickey and Ivan sprinted through the forest.

For a moment, it seemed the two boys would escape. But then two cougars burst into view in front of them!

In seconds, Ivan and Mickey were surrounded.

"Quick!" the Quiet Prince shouted. "Climb that tree!"

Ivan shimmied up fast. Mickey was right behind him. Soon, the two boys were perched on branches, staring down at six cougars.

"Like a pack of dogs cornering a raccoon," one of the cougars said.

"That reminds me," said another. "Why do dogs run in circles?"

"Easy!" shouted a third. "Because it's hard to run in squares!"

They howled with laughter. Ivan pulled up his earmuffs.

The cougars looked at him and shrugged.

They started throwing spears! One of them thudded into the tree trunk right beside Ivan's head!

Then a miracle happened.

All around the cougars, a dozen little green elves *stepped out of the trees*, emerging from the trunks! They all had grassy hair and deep brown eyes. Moss and leaves covered them like clothing.

"What are they?" Ivan asked Mickey.

"They're chaneks," he replied. "Forest spirits. Oh, it is on now!"

The chaneks lifted their green hands and made a sweeping movement. The woods came to life! Branches swayed and smacked two of the cougars. Vines whipped through the air and snatched another pair up, wrapping around them like ropes. Roots tripped the two that tried to run away, and as they hit the ground, grass quickly grew over their bodies, trapping them.

Mickey looked at Ivan. "See? They got 'em!"

CHAPTER

11

CHANEKS AND CATNIP

The chaneks made the cougars fall asleep with the magic catnip powder Mickey had used to free Ivan. Then Mickey led Ivan and the elves deeper into what he called "the Weird Wood."

"Where are we going?" Ivan asked.

"To the chaneks' village," Mickey explained.

The wooded area of the park wasn't that big.

In just a few minutes, they reached a cave hollowed out in the cliff on the edge. Gardens of herbs and mushrooms spread out in semi-circles. Chaneks silently tended to the plants.

It was a calm paradise. But Ivan's mind wasn't calm at all. He couldn't stop thinking about his cousins, hypnotized, having to obey every command of a bunch of cackling cougars.

He thought back to the moment when he had wished he was all alone on the mountain and imagined life without Malia and Dante. Sure, they had little in common, and sometimes they made him feel like he didn't belong. But they were his family. He could always lean on Malia, and Dante could always make him laugh.

Ivan couldn't let anything happen to them!

"Why are they after us?" he demanded.

"To train you," Mickey replied, his voice cracking. "To make you dogcatchers."

Ivan felt that sinking feeling again. "We have to rescue them, and you're going to help me."

"Of course," he replied.

"Where are the cougars taking them?" Ivan asked.

"They've set up camp beyond the woods," the Quiet Prince explained, "on the other side of the park."

Ivan glanced at the chaneks who had saved him. They were crouched over some flowers, watching the bees.

"Excuse me, how much of that catnip do you have?"

Looking up, they sang a single word in unison: "Mi-yak."

"A lot," Mickey translated.

"Good," Ivan said. "We're going to need it all."

Whoa. What's going to happen next? Only four more chapters left!

CHAPTER

12

TRICKY TRAINING

Captain Kamak stood in front of the command tent, looking at Dante and Malia.

"Okay, newbies," Kamak said. "If my scouts find paw prints, we'll be sending you in. Dogs like humans better than cougars. If you find Bruno, call to him. When he gets close, you collar him. Then do the whistle I taught you. Lieutenant Ezzy?"

One of the knights put a silver collar in Malia's hand.

"Today you practice," the captain explained. "Boy cub, you're the dog. Run off toward those swings and hide."

Dante couldn't stop himself. He dropped to all fours and hurried toward a twisted, rusted playground.

Kamak laughed. "Okay. Girl cub, you're the dogcatcher. Go collar that mutt!"

Malia felt her legs move. She began to follow her cousin's trail, handprints and knee marks in the muddy ground. A few yards behind her came Lieutenant Ezzy, yawning.

"Yay," the cougar muttered. "Watching human cubs."

Dante had ducked into some bushes near the swings. Suddenly, he felt a hand on his shoulder.

It was Ivan, shoving a healing stone against his chest.

"Heal up, Shi-PAH-ti!" he whispered.

Dante's eyes opened wide! He was about to speak, but Ivan put his finger to his lips so he'd stay quiet.

Just then, Malia walked past the swings, her head swiveling back and forth. She saw the marks leading to the bushes. Holding the silver collar tight, she leaned in.

As fast as he could, Ivan freed her from hypnosis! She started to pull back, but he shook his head.

"Wait!" he said softly. "Act like you're still hypnotized. They can't suspect a thing, okay?"

CHAPTER

13

COUGAR CAMP

A few minutes later, Ivan walked into the cougar camp, the silver collar around his neck. Lieutenant Ezzy held a spear to his back. Dante and Malia pretended to shuffle like zombies at his side.

Captain Kamak grinned. "That's no dog, but good job, newbies! Now take him to the mess tent. He can help clean up after lunch. Ezzy, come here. I want a full report."

Malia pulled on Ivan's collar, leading him away. They soon came to a spot between tents where no one could see them.

Without warning, Ivan grabbed his cousins and hugged them tightly.

"Whoa!" said Malia, squirming. Dante squeezed him back.

"I'm just glad you're okay," Ivan said. "Though you didn't have to tighten the collar so much, Malia." He unbuckled the collar and tossed it away.

"You said to make it look real," Malia reminded him.

Dante pulled away, smiling. "Dude, I'm sorry about before. I should have believed you in the beginning."

"Me too," Malia said. "You only wanted to protect us."

"Thanks, guys." Ivan smiled. Maybe they understood him more than he realized.

"So what's the plan?" Dante asked.

"We need to get them all together in a small space," Ivan said. "Then we can use catnip dust to make them sleepy. Our portal opens, and boom! We're back in the snow."

"I say we use their own mission against them," said Malia.

Dante slapped his hands together. "I love it! We'll put their training to use."

"But wait," Malia said. "You don't have any catnip with you, Ivan. Ezzy searched you."

Ivan smiled. "Don't worry. We've got some awesome friends!"

CHAPTER

14

NIGHTY NIGHT!

"What are you hairless apes doing?" It was an old cougar carrying a bucket full of stinky red meat. "Why aren't you hypnotized?"

As hard as he could, Ivan kicked the bucket. "Protect us, Shi-YA-na!"

With a **WHOOSH**, Mickey Aguilar appeared. He was holding a big bag and two snowboards.

"His Bratty Majesty!" snarled the old cougar, leaping to attack.

"Oh, great," Mickey said, dropping everything and using his cape to disappear.

"What a jerk!" Dante groaned. "Always leaving right when we—"

Mickey reappeared right behind the old cougar and shoved it to the ground, sitting on its chest. "Hurry! Throw some of the catnip at it!"

"How?!" Malia picked up the bag, sticking her hand inside.

The old cougar was snapping its jaws at the Quiet Prince, trying to bite him.

"Like this!" Mickey clamped his hands on either side of its face. "Open, Hebaan!"

The cougar's mouth popped open! Malia flung her handful of catnip at it. Within seconds, the cougar was snoring.

"Where are the rest of them?" Mickey asked, wiping sweat from his forehead.

Malia put two fingers to her lips and whistled. The sound was loud and piercing.

"On their way," she said.

Holding out the bag, Mickey spilled the catnip around them in a circle.

Just then, the Knights of the Quiet Prince came running toward them from all directions. Dozens of cougars, snarling.

"On my signal, slap your hands against the ground," Mickey told them, "and shout, 'Rise up, SHE-wa!' Okay?"

"Where's the dog, human cubs?" one of the

cougars hissed.

"Where? Where?" the others repeated, getting closer and closer, brandishing claws and spears.

"Now!" shouted Mickey.

The cousins dropped to their knees beside him and slammed their palms against the ground. "**RISE UP, SHE-WA!**"

The catnip was blown up into the air and out toward the cougars.

Almost in unison, the knights dropped to the ground, asleep.

Malia stood, looking over her shoulder. "Where's the portal? Why hasn't it appeared?"

"Because we're still standing!" The kids spun around. Captain Kamak and Lieutenant Ezzy were approaching, furious. "What've you done, brats?"

"We gave your troop catnip," Dante said. "Not very bright, are you? Hey, Ivan, what do you call a cougar with half a brain?"

Ivan smiled. "Gifted?"

"Boom!" Dante laughed. "Feel the burn, kitty cat."

The captain smiled. "Not bad. Now I'll laugh you into submission."

Ivan and Malia reached for their earmuffs. Dante shoved his fingers in his ears.

Then **BOOM**! The ground behind the cougars exploded upward. Roots and vines snaked out of the hole and grabbed the two knights. Three chaneks stepped out of the biggest root. They lifted their hands to their lips and blew catnip powder into the struggling cougars' faces.

"Shi-ko-chi-kan," they sang.

"Ha! Nighty night," Mickey translated.

The cougars' eyes closed.

WHAM! A portal popped open! Through the glowing circle, Ivan could make out the snowy slope of a mountain. "Dante, Malia—time to leave!"

Ivan touched the Quiet Prince's arm. "Come on, Mickey. I think your grandmother *really* misses you. Maybe she's been hoping we'd find you."

Mickey turned, tears in his eyes. "I can't. I came for my dog. My portal won't open until I find him."

One more chapter and we're home! But don't worry about Mickey. Confien en mi. That means trust me!

CHAPTER

15

DOWN THE SLOPE AT LAST

"The portal's closing, dude!" Dante shouted. He and Malia had already strapped on their snowboards.

Ivan nodded. "Right behind y'all!"

Malia and Dante jumped through the portal onto the snowy slope.

"Go," Mickey said. "I'll be fine."

Ivan dove, belly flopping onto the snow. It was a cold and fast ride down the slope.

Finally, he reached the bottom and shook frost from his face.

Dante gingerly touched his hair, which was miraculously perfect despite their adventure. "And Mickey?"

"I think our portal wouldn't work for him," Ivan explained. "To return, he has to find Bruno."

The cousins stared at one another in silence until Dr. Eisenberg, Ivan's father, came trudging across the snow with mugs of hot chocolate.

"Ivan?" he called. "What happened to your skis?"

"I got mugged, Dad," Ivan explained. "Some guy with a spear."

Panicked, his father yanked out his phone and called the police.

As he walked away, Malia groaned in frustration.

"I can't believe I'm saying this," she muttered, "but we can't leave him there."

Dante shook his head. "Boss, no."

Ivan stood, brushing snow from his pants. "She's right, Dante. We have to go back and help."

CONGRATULATIONS!

You've read **15** chapters,

87 pages,

and **5,078** words!

MAD RESPECT!

ACTIVITIES

THINK!

The cousins are hypnotized and have to obey commands. Think about the choices you've made on your own today.

FEEL!

Malia and Dante don't believe Ivan's theory about 13th Street. When you aren't believed, how does that make you feel?

ACT!

The cousins meet a new friend on 13th Street. Make a list of ways to welcome new kids at school and in your neighborhood.

Photo by Paul Chouy

DAVID BOWLES is the award-winning Mexican American author of many books for young readers. He's traveled all over Mexico studying creepy legends, exploring ancient ruins, and avoiding monsters (so far). He lives in Donna, Texas.

Courtesy Shane Clester

SHANE CLESTER has been a professional illustrator since 2005, working on comics, storyboards, and children's books. Shane lives in Florida with his wonderful wife and their two tots. When not illustrating, he can usually be found by the pool.